Grumpy Bear

Best Friend Bear

Secret Bear

This book belongs to:

Signy

Wish Bear

Love-a-lot Bear

Published by Scholastic Inc.
90 Old Sherman Turnpike, Danbury, CT 06816.

SCHOLASTIC and associated logos are trademarks and/or registered trademarks of Scholastic Inc.

ISBN 0-439-79992-9

First Scholastic Printing, January 2006

A Fun-Shiny Day

by
Nancy Parent
& Quinlan B. Lee

Illustrated by
David Stein &
Rivoli Design Group

SCHOLASTIC INC.

New York   Toronto   London   Auckland   Sydney
Mexico City   New Delhi   Hong Kong   Buenos Aires

It was a sunny day in Care-a-lot, but the Care Bears weren't feeling very sunny.

"I am bored," sighed Grumpy Bear.

"I wish there was something fun to do," said Wish Bear. "We've played all these games before."

7

"I know what would be fun!" said Funshine Bear. "Let's have a Caring Contest. I will give a prize to the bear who shows the best way to care."

First Annual
Care-a-lot
Caring Contest

The Care Bears took the contest very seriously. Secret Bear was the first to think of a way to care.

"It's no secret that caring means . . . taking turns with a favorite toy," she said.

9

10

Share Bear cared by making sure she had enough treats for everyone.

"Help yourself!"
she said as she passed out
yummy rainbow bars.

When Wish Bear wanted a push
on her swing, Best Friend Bear was there.

"Caring is being there when someone needs help," said Wish Bear.

Best Friend Bear laughed. "And helping is what best friends do best!" she said.

During an afternoon storm, Grumpy Bear saw a way to care for Bashful Heart Bear. "Caring," said Grumpy Bear, "is sharing your umbrella in the rain."

When Share Bear didn't feel well,
some of her friends visited her.

"Comforting someone who's sick

shows you really care," said Love-a-lot Bear.

"Caring is making someone laugh when he's sad," said Cheer Bear.

So she juggled stars to cheer up Grumpy Bear.

19

"I can show I care by letting you go ahead of me in line," Wish Bear told Love-a-lot Bear. "I'd love to!" said Love-a-lot Bear. "Thanks!"

When Wish Bear
couldn't fall asleep at naptime,
Bedtime Bear read her a sweet
dreams story to show he cared.

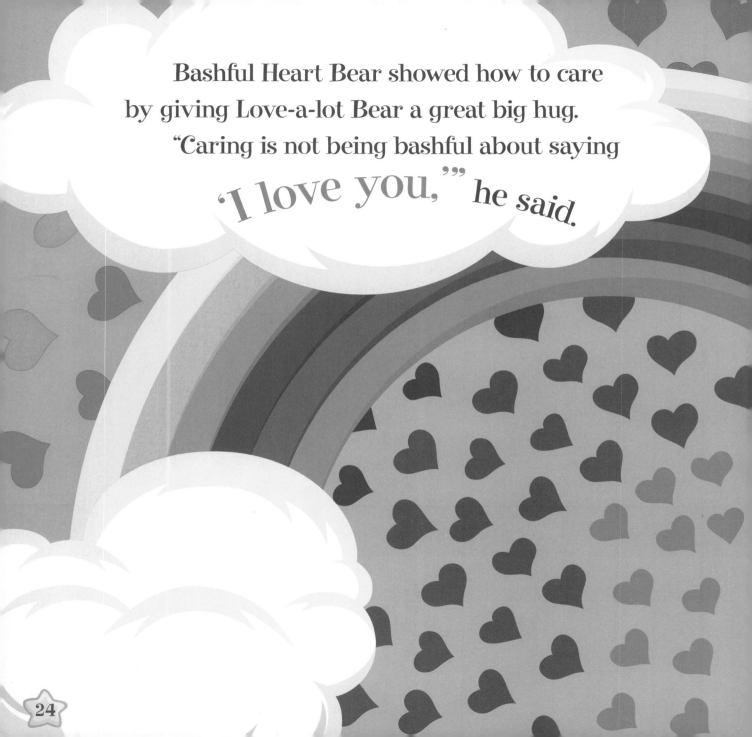

Bashful Heart Bear showed how to care
by giving Love-a-lot Bear a great big hug.
"Caring is not being bashful about saying
'I love you,'" he said.

24

Funshine Bear thought
all the Care Bears had done
a wonderful job of caring.
But who should he pick as
the winner of the contest?

First Annual
Care-a-lot
Caring Contest

Care-a-lot Caring Contest

"I was wrong," said Funshine Bear.
"This isn't fun!
It's too hard to decide
who should win."

But then Funshine Bear had an idea—a great
idea about how to keep the fun going.

Funshine Bear made an announcement:
"The winners of the Care-a-lot Caring Contest are—

all of you!

Because everyone
wins when everyone
cares for others!"

Then he proudly handed out the prizes.

"Now we can show how much we care by sharing these prizes with our friends!" all the Care Bears said together.

"Sounds like fun to me!"
cheered Funshine Bear.

That night, all of the
Care Bears were tired
when Bedtime Bear
tucked them in.

"I was wrong," said Wish Bear.
"This day turned out to be really fun."

"Of course," said Funshine Bear with a sleepy smile.

"Any day you spend caring is sure to be fun!"

35

How Can You Make Caring Fun Like Funshine Bear?

At first, some of the Care Bears were bored.

♥ Are you ever bored?

♥ Does it make you feel happy or sad?

♥ What could you do the next time you feel bored?

If you were in a Caring Contest like
the Care Bears, what would you do?
💜 What's your favorite way
to show someone you care?

Do you think it's fun to show you care?
💜 When have you had a good time
helping someone else?

Bashful Heart Bear

Cheer Bear

Share Bear

Bedtime Bear

Funshine Bear